ROBIN·HOOD

PAUL CRESWICK
illustrated by N.C.WYETH

A SCRIBNER STORYBOOK CLASSIC
Atheneum Books for Young Readers
New York London Toronto Sydney Singapore

Atheneum Books for Young Readers

An imprint of Simon & Schuster Children's Publishing Division

1230 Avenue of the Americas

New York, New York 10020

Book design by Abelardo Martinez

The text of this book is set in Palatino.

The illustrations are rendered in oil.

Manufactured in China

First Edition

2 4 6 8 10 9 7 5 3 1

Library of Congress Cataloging-in-Publication Data

Creswick, Paul, 1866-1947.

Robin Hood : a Scribner storybook classic / Paul Creswick ; illustrated by N. C. Wyeth.—1st ed.

p.   cm. — (a Scribner storybook classic ; 4)

Summary: An abridged version of the legend of Robin Hood, who plundered the king's purse
and poached his deer, and whose generosity endeared him to the poor.

ISBN 0-689-85467-6

1. Robin Hood (Legendary character)—Legends. [1. Robin Hood (Legendary character)—Legends.

2. Folklore—England.] I. Wyeth, N. C. (Newell Convers), 1882-1945, ill. II. Title. III. Series.

PZ8.1.C876Rp 2003

[Fic]—dc21   2002153750

PROLOGUE

*I*n the year of Our Lord 1190, Prince Richard Plantagenet, son of King Henry II of England, sailed for the Holy Land to free Jerusalem from Saladin, the sultan of the Moors. A brave and noble man, Richard fought alongside his soldiers upon the hot sands of Palestine. While besieging the Accursed Tower at the Battle of Acre, Richard was struck by an arrow.

He fell from his horse before the eyes of his entire army. His men rushed from their attacking positions to save him. But Richard, knowing the day would be lost if they abandoned the siege, plucked the arrow from his chest with one hand. He mounted his horse, held the arrow aloft, and led his men to victory.

It was upon that day that the legend of Richard the Lionheart began. Stories of Richard's bravery soon made their way to England, the prince's ancestral home.

The arrow, made from a shaft of polished ebony wood and the brilliant turquoise and purple feathers of a peacock, was said to have almost magical properties. So perfectly was it made, that once set across a bow, it almost always found its mark. For it had been fashioned by the greatest arrow maker in Palestine for Saladin, who shot it from nearly half a battlefield away at the English prince. And after it had been dipped in the blood of Plantagenet royalty, this Moorish arrow was rumored to possess the very strength of Richard himself. Victory after victory was won by Richard, who carried the ebony and peacock feather dart into every battle. And soon all of the Holy Land, save for Jerusalem herself, fell before his conquering army.

But all was not well at home in England. Word had reached Richard that his younger brother, Prince John, was positioning himself to take the throne when their father, King Henry II, died. John lacked Richard's noble and kind heart, and the English people did not like how he overtaxed their properties and worse, kept the money for himself. The people became poorer as Prince John and those loyal to him became richer. Instead of a free people, Englishmen were beginning to feel like slaves as John attempted to seize more and more power.

Having learned of this injustice, Richard hoped that his father would put things right. But King Henry, old and ailing, had little strength to fight his younger son. Knowing he could not leave the Holy Land until he captured Jerusalem, Richard called for his most trusted friend, William Fitzooth. William had fought, and was wounded, beside the prince and had proven himself to be both brave and honorable.

Richard instructed his old friend to return to England and rally men of the countryside to the cause of freedom against Prince John's villainy. He took his peacock arrow, wrapped it in a kerchief that bore his royal seal—three lions upon a scarlet field—and gave it to William. If any doubted that William traveled in Richard's name, he was told to show them the arrow.

And so William Fitzooth set off for England. Prince Richard, however, did not capture the prize of Jerusalem. It seemed that without the arrow to lead them into battle, the men of the Third Crusade faltered on their march to that Holy City.

William Fitzooth did return to England, but did not rally any men to Richard's cause of freedom. He died of the wounds he received in the Holy Land soon after arriving home.

Believing his older brother would never return from the Holy Land to oppose him, Prince John continued to seize more and more land and money from the peasants, and soon they began to hate him.

And the arrow that had been drawn out of Richard the Lionheart's breast passed to William Fitzooth's son, Robin.

CHAPTER ONE

"At last!" Robin Fitzooth exclaimed to his mother, bringing his horse up alongside hers as they rode through Sherwood Forest toward the city of Nottingham.

"Yes, at last," his mother said, smiling at her eager son. "You are finally old enough to enter the archery tournament."

"And show all of Sherwood who the greatest archer in the land is," Robin added, standing in his stirrups, barely able to contain his excitement. He prodded his horse on faster with a clucking of his tongue, but his guardian, Warrenton, who rode nearby with the rest of the caravan of travelers, called to him.

"You best keep close," Warrenton warned. "More than one traveler has been robbed or killed by highwaymen along this route."

The road to Nottingham wound in and about Sherwood Forest. The forest was a wide expanse of trees, glens, and hills where a thief could easily hide before springing on his prey. And since her husband, William Fitzooth, had died, Dame Fitzooth had become overly protective of her only son, Robin. She made sure Warrenton rarely left her son's side.

But Robin felt no threat in Sherwood, and at sixteen, he felt he was too old for a guardian. It was among these wooded glens that he spent most of his youth. The lands of his home, Locksley, and Sherwood Forest lay back to back, and he knew each root, cave, rock, and tree within them.

"How long before we reach the fair?" he asked.

"Not long," his mother replied, glancing uneasily from side to side.

"And not long before I show Prince Richard's peacock arrow to all of Nottingham," Robin said.

"Robin, I told you to leave that arrow at home! You must be more modest about your talent, and more careful with the peacock arrow. Your father valued that arrow more than any of his other possessions. You and it were all he spoke about before he passed from this life."

"Don't worry, Mother. I'm only carrying it for good luck. Perhaps its magic will rub off on my other arrows."

"Just be sure to keep it in your quiver. Who knows how the Sheriff of Nottingham would react if he saw Richard's arrow. He could well tell Prince John, and they could look on us as traitors and take away your father's estate."

"If Father were still alive," Robin declared, "we would have no need to fear the Sheriff *or* Prince John."

"Even if your father were still here, one man is not an army," his mother said. "Richard hasn't been heard from in over a year, and no man dares stand against Prince John. Freedom has no leader in our land."

Robin looked pensively at his mother. "It will some day," he said to himself.

The road to Nottingham wound in and about Sherwood Forest.

CHAPTER TWO

The Sheriff of Nottingham could announce a fair whenever he fancied, but there was usually an occasion. Sometimes it would be to show the town's finery to a visiting earl or a prince, sometimes to celebrate a wedding, and sometimes, such as on this day, to celebrate the first of May and the beginning of spring in the county. Or at least that was the reason he gave the people. For the Sheriff was not a kind man, and everything that he did, he did for himself.

"I've heard rumors that Prince Richard's peacock arrow has been sighted in Sherwood Forest. One of my foresters told me he witnessed a deer being felled by it," the Sheriff had said to his second-in-command, Lord Carfax, a few days before the fair. "If he has returned from the Holy Land, I must know immediately. If anyone else fires the arrow, I want him killed." As he spoke the Sheriff held out pieces of raw meat to the falcon that perched upon his gloved hand. The bird tore them from his grasp.

"Killed?" Carfax asked, his cold eyes remaining fixed on the bird as it devoured the bloody flesh.

"That is the only way to ensure there will be no threat when Prince John takes the throne," the Sheriff told him. "Even the slightest rumor of Richard's return could cause the people to rebel. So the one who fires the arrow must be . . ."

"Killed," repeated Carfax, smiling.

As Robin, his mother, Warrenton, and the other traveling companions who made their way to the fair passed through Nottingham's north gate, Robin's attention was drawn to a wrestling match. A crowd had gathered around to watch a boy Robin's age grappling with older, stronger men and throwing them to the ground. Robin gaped at the boy, astonished.

The lads were quickly upon each other.

"Mother," Robin said quickly, "go on ahead. I will meet you at the archery field. I want to watch this for a moment."

"Go on, Dame Fitzooth," Warrenton assured her. "Find a place to watch the competition, and I'll stay with Robin."

Once his mother had departed, Robin hopped off his horse. He waited for the young wrestler to take a break, then he spoke up.

"You must have some trick," he said.

"There is no trick," replied the boy, dusting off his hands. "I am the best in the county, and I can throw any man."

"That sounds to me like a challenge," Robin said, putting down his bow and quiver. The lads were quickly upon each other. Though Robin maneuvered well, he was no match for the quick reflexes and strong muscles of the young wrestler. Robin soon found himself thrown face-first into the mud. He laughed at the dirt on his chest, and the other boy laughed along with him.

"You are a worthy opponent, for a lad my size," said the wrestler. "I am Will Stuteley. What is your name?"

"I am Robin of Locksley," Robin announced, grasping Will's arm with affection. "Teach me how you do that!"

"Gladly," said Stuteley, sensing that he had found a new friend. "And what can you teach me?"

"I am the greatest archer in all of Britain," Robin announced with a grin. He tried to wipe off the mud from the front of his leather jerkin, but only succeeded in smearing it more.

"Then you must be here to enter the archery tournament," Stuteley said. "If you win there, then come back and I will show you what I know."

"First, young man," Warrenton chided Robin, "you should change into fresh clothes."

Robin looked at his mud-spattered outfit and agreed. "Perhaps you are right.

Fetch me my satchel; I brought my new birthday outfit—the one with the hood—and I can change behind the wall here," he said, and began removing his shoes.

Robin and Warrenton approached the archery fields, which were resplendent in banners, bunting, pennants, and the brightly-colored dresses of the noblewomen and girls who were in attendance. The weather was warm, and the flags hoisted high above barely flickered in the slight breeze. The Sheriff of Nottingham had already taken his place of honor in the centermost tent's viewing stand.

As Robin made his way across the field, his eye caught sight of a beautiful raven-haired girl who sat smiling at him. She was dressed in a sky-blue velvet robe and a red cape the color of fresh roses. To Robin, she seemed the essence of spring itself.

He couldn't stop himself from walking over to her tent. He paused in front of her. "What is your name?" he asked.

"Marian Fitzwalter," she replied, blushing.

Robin smiled broadly as he pushed back his green hood. "My name is Robin."

Marian grinned and said teasingly, "Robin o' th' Hood?"

Robin laughed at the joke, but before he could answer her, the horn for the archery tournament sounded. "I'm sorry, but I must go. We will meet again," he said hurriedly. "And I pray it will be soon."

"Take this for luck," she said, handing him a simple white linen handkerchief with the initials MF embroidered on it. Robin tucked it into his pocket.

"Thank you, Maid Marian. I will return it to you after I win," he said. Then he turned and trotted out onto the field with the other competitors.

Nearly two dozen archers shot at round wooden targets, which had been cut from the trunk of an elm tree. After each round, the targets were set back

another fifty paces. As the tournament progressed on into the afternoon there were but a handful of archers left competing. Robin, steady and sure with his bow of yew wood and arrows fashioned from the limb of an ash tree, shot well, and by the final round only he and Lord Carfax remained.

"You're a fine shot," Robin said as the target was being moved back to four hundred paces.

"The best in England," Carfax said disdainfully, not bothering to so much as glance at the younger man. He tightened the string on his longbow.

Robin looked at him curiously. The Sheriff's emblem, the falcon and dagger, was inscribed on his coat. "I see you shoot for the Sheriff of Nottingham," Robin said.

"What is that to you?" Carfax replied. "Under whose banner do you stand?"

Robin very much wanted to say, "Richard, the rightful heir of the English throne," but he remembered his mother's warning. So instead he said, "Freedom's banner."

Carfax pulled an arrow from his quiver and drew it across his bow. "Freedom!" He laughed. But the laugh was not friendly. He released his grip and let the arrow soar. It found its mark in the red spot at the target's center. The crowd roared.

"You can not score better than a direct bull's-eye!" Carfax said proudly as his arrow reverberated slightly in the center of the target. "No need to continue the tournament, is there?"

Robin drew in a breath and thought for a moment. To give up now would prove that this other man was the better archer. He couldn't bear that. But he also knew there was only one way to improve upon Carfax's shot. The only chance he had was to use the arrow he had never missed with—the peacock arrow.

Robin drew two arrows from his quiver: Richard's arrow, and a common arrow of ash wood to hide the ebony dart. He then let the ash wand drop to the ground as he set the peacock arrow upon his bowstring. He looked down

Marian grinned and said teasingly, "Robin o' th' Hood?"

its shaft from the turquoise peacock feathers that shimmered in the sunlight to the tip set directly at the target.

As if repeating a magic spell, he whispered to it, "As you once flew at Prince Richard's heart, now find the heart of Carfax's arrow." He drew the bowstring back till his hand touched his shoulder. Then, as if the dart had a mind of its own, it sprung from his hand with purpose and force. The speed at which it cut the air caused the arrow to whistle loudly before it struck the target with a mighty crack, and for a hushed moment, the crowd stared. Robin raised his bow in victory. Not only did he score a direct hit, he had split Carfax's arrow directly down the center, shattering it. He'd won!

Carfax stepped back, amazed and angry. "You'll regret bettering me," he hissed to Robin as the younger man set out to retrieve his peacock arrow.

Robin thought the man a very poor sport, and turned from him to instead acknowledge the crowd's applause by waving the arrow over his head. Then he gasped, realizing what he had done. He quickly stuck the arrow back into the quiver, but it was too late.

Carfax recognized the arrow and shouted over the green, "He shoots Richard's arrow!"

Robin turned to see the Sheriff bellowing at his soldiers. They drew their swords and ran at Robin.

"Run!" Warrenton yelled out to Robin from the side of the field. "Head for the north gate; it's the nearest exit." Robin wasted no time departing the green, slowing only to call to his mother.

"Return to Locksley," Robin said. "I will meet you there." Dame Fitzooth watched for a moment in horror as a dozen of the Sheriff's men pounded after her son, then gathered up her dress and made for her horse.

As Robin raced from the village center and approached the gate, he ran into Will Stuteley, nearly knocking the young wrestler over.

"Why the hurry, Robin?" Will called, grabbing his arm.

Robin laughed, for he found the chase thrilling and invigorating. "There is adventure afoot, Stuteley! Will you join me?"

Stuteley turned to see the Sheriff's men round the corner at a full run. He grinned. "A merry chase!" he shouted. "Let the wind try and catch us!" And together they sped off through the gate and into the countryside, never once pausing to look behind them.

CHAPTER THREE

*R*obin hid in the greenwood of Sherwood Forest for two nights with his newfound friend Will Stuteley. He taught Stuteley all he knew about being a forester: how the call of the drake signals rain, how the edible moss only grows on the eastern face of a tree, and which snort of a female deer signals that it is soon to give birth.

And though Robin knew the Sheriff's men were probably still searching for him, he little expected the shock he received when he finally returned to Locksley. As he and Stuteley exited the forest and made their way to his manor house, the smell of fresh smoke permeated the air.

Without a word Robin broke into a run, sprinting the distance back to the house. As he crested the hill he saw Warrenton, covered in soot. Then Robin saw that beyond him Locksley Manor was in flames.

"My mother?" Robin gasped. "Is she all right?"

"She has taken in a great deal of smoke," Warrenton replied, "but she was able to sneak out the back and is heading for town with her handmaiden." He looked Robin steadily in the eye and then told him, "One of the Sheriff's men, the one you shot against, ordered her to vacate Locksley. When she would not, he set fire to it to force her out."

"String your bow, my friend," Robin told Stuteley as he once again broke into a run.

"Stop, Robin!" Warrenton shouted after him, but it was too late. Robin was already halfway to the house. Warrenton had no choice but to follow him.

Robin was sickened as he approached his home. Nearly a dozen of the Sheriff's soldiers were sweeping around the area with torches, making sure every last part of the estate, from the stables to the garden house, was afire. And the soldiers who weren't torching the exterior were busy looting the interior—man after man exited the manor with his arms full of gowns and furs, gold candlesticks and fine oak furniture. In the orange glow of the fire, Robin thought they looked like demons stealing away with the riches of his inheritance.

The men were so preoccupied that Robin was easily able to sneak up on them. His arrows found one man, then two, and then a third. All fell before they could even draw a shaft of an arrow from their quivers. The remaining soldiers, alarmed and surprised, dropped their torches and reached for their bows. While half of them turned and shot at Robin and Stuteley, the other half raced around the house for their horses, anxious to avoid the quick succession of the boys' arrows. These men were met by Warrenton, who caught them by surprise with his heavy wood quarterstaff, sending them scurrying into the house for protection. Warrenton quickly slammed his quarterstaff in front of the door, blocking their escape. Within moments the burning roof collapsed, burying the men inside under a heap of scorching cinder.

Before he lost any more of his soldiers, Carfax wheeled his horse around and ordered them to withdraw. Thick, dark, pungent smoke filled the sky, casting a shadow over the heartbroken Robin. By the time he put down his bow, Locksley Manor, his father's house, had burned to the ground.

CHAPTER FOUR

*R*obin did not find his mother in town, but on a patch of grass by the roadside, barely halfway there, coughing violently. Her handmaiden called urgently to Robin as he approached.

"Mistress Fitzooth has taken in too much smoke from the fire; she's very weak," she said, her voice quavering.

Robin knelt over his mother and wiped the soot from her forehead. "Mother," he said softly. And again, "Mother."

She looked up, and a faint smile came to her lips. With labored breath she said, "I feared you were dead these past few days. Praise be to God you're not."

"I hid in the greenwood, Mother," Robin said breathlessly, "hoping the Sheriff would continue searching for me and leave you and our home alone."

"Warrenton and I couldn't defend Locksley against Carfax's soldiers," she gasped, gripping Robin by the hand.

"Be still, Mother. I will seek revenge for what the Sheriff has done," Robin said to her, cradling her head in his hands. She coughed violently, then closed her eyes.

"Mother!" he cried. But her eyes remained shut.

For a long time Robin remained on his knees beside her, hoping against hope that she would draw another breath, but she did not. A lone tear fell from his eye, leaving a clear line through the soot that darkened her face.

When at last he stood, both Warrenton and Stuteley were waiting nearby. He looked at them with a face full of anguish and fury.

"The Sheriff sent Carfax to murder my mother and burn and loot our property for no reason," Robin said, his voice shaking with anger. "Let us see how he responds to being robbed and having his soldiers killed! I will do what my father was unable to do: take up Prince Richard's cause of freedom."

"Robin," Stuteley said, grasping his shoulder. "If you intend to be an outlaw, I'll join you. But what can we do against the Sheriff's army?"

"Behold," Robin said as he drew out an arrow and slung it across his bow. Ahead of them was the Bishop of Hereford, dressed in a cloak of purple satin trimmed with gold buttons, riding up the road, followed by two young attendants.

"Halt!" Robin shouted, aiming the arrow at the Bishop's neck.

"A highwayman!" gasped the cleric.

"I would have known the sound of the Bishop of Hereford's approach from miles away," Robin said evenly as he approached the portly rider. "You make your steed sink near to its knees with your weight. Or perhaps it is the weight of the gold you carry that makes your horse's hooves so heavy upon the road."

Without lowering his bow, Robin turned to Stuteley and said, "It is well known in the county that the bishop takes from the poor boxes of his church and lives like a king with the gold. See how he dresses. And see how his purse bulges."

Robin, turning back to the bishop and pointing to the money pouch dangling from the bishop's belt, said, "You should let me distribute this money for you."

"This is an outrage! You cannot steal from me!" the bishop roared, regaining his composure. "I travel on the business of Prince John and ride to see the Sheriff of Nottingham. Rob me, and he will hear about it."

"That is what I intend," Robin said with a knowing smile.

After Robin let the bishop and his two attendants go, he passed the purse of gold to his mother's handmaiden.

"You have been faithful to my mother for many years," Robin told her. "Take this and find yourself a place in town to live. And tell those you meet that they no longer need to live in fear of the Sheriff." Then he turned to Stuteley.

"We will live here in Sherwood Forest and lighten the purses of the rich and proud who travel through it. It will be a tough life, my friend, but we will be free. From this day onward," he continued, "I bind myself to Prince Richard and the cause of freedom."

"I do as well," said Will Stuteley.

"And I," replied Warrenton.

"For Richard! The true heir," Robin said, grabbing his friends by the shoulders.

"For Richard!" the two men shouted.

"And for freedom for all Englishmen."

"For freedom!"

CHAPTER FIVE

*T*he ranks of the freemen of the greenwood, as Robin's troop called themselves, grew slowly. As stories circulated among the townsfolk about a band of merry men in Sherwood Forest who stole from the rich and gave to the poor, men who chafed under the cruel rule of the Sheriff of Nottingham ventured into Sherwood and sought the freemen out.

Soon the band included Robin, Stuteley, Warrenton, Allan-a-Dale, a farmer who had had his land taken, Will Scarlett, an ex-knight from Tickhill Castle, Arthur-à-Bland from nearby Lincolnshire, Middle the Tinker, Much the Miller, and a cook named Roger who claimed he once prepared meals for the Sheriff himself. Roger was a quiet man, not given to laughing and singing with the other men. And though Robin found this behavior strange, Roger's skill at preparing succulent deer and pheasant feasts more than made up for his lack of conversation.

One bright morning in early spring Robin was hunting deer in the northern woods. As he crossed the bridge near St. Dunstan's Chapel he encountered an exceptionally tall, ungainly man with a rough beard. The bridge was narrow, and the tall man made no attempt to move aside to allow Robin to pass.

"Ho there, friend," Robin said with a smile, "this is a bridge for all free men."

"Out of my way, little one," said the man gruffly. "I have business to be about and I desire to be on my way."

"And I desire to hold a dark-haired maiden with gray-blue eyes that I once met at a fair," Robin countered with a laugh. "But desiring it will not make it so."

"Spare me your tales of love, little man. You are free to pursue your maiden, and I am free to cross this bridge, so step aside."

Robin did not like the man's tone so he held up his palm to the man's chest, stopping him.

"*Are* you a freeman?" Robin asked, his voice becoming more serious.

"I am as free as any other man in Nottingham," replied the man.

"Then you are not free at all," Robin answered back.

"I am free," the man said as he drew out his wooden cudgel, "to wallop you about the head."

Robin stepped back. "If it is a fight you want, then a fight you shall have. First let me find an equal weapon." He cut a branch from a nearby elm with his knife and quickly fashioned a crude cudgel. Then he stepped forward and struck first.

But the tall man was surprisingly swift with his weapon, parrying Robin's thrust with a quick jab of his own. He caught Robin beneath the arm and tried to throw him from the bridge, but Robin swung his cudgel and landed a heavy blow upon the man's thigh. As the man clutched his leg Robin drew his cudgel back for a final whack. But at that moment the man, using his head, butted Robin off the bridge and into the stream.

Robin thrashed about in the frigid water, frantically looking for his cudgel, when he saw his opponent standing over him, knee-deep in the stream.

"You should have let me pass to find the freemen of the greenwood whom I seek," the towering man bellowed. And as he brought back his cudgel for a final blow, Robin whistled a distinctive three quick notes. In but a moment Robin's men, alerted by his call, stood by the stream with arrows drawn.

The man looked about in surprise and thrust his cudgel back into his belt.

"It is good that you have friends, little man!" he said with a laugh.

"In truth," Robin replied, "I would be pleased to be blessed with another." He offered his hand to his opponent, who accepted it. With a heavy yank, he pulled Robin out of the water and onto the mossy bank of

In but a moment Robin's men, alerted by his call, stood by the stream with arrows drawn.

the stream. Robin thanked him and said, "My name is Robin Fitzooth, formerly of Locksley."

"Robin of Locksley! I have not heard that name since your house was burned after you bested the Sheriff's man on the archery green. The rumor was that you died in the fire."

"Died?" Robin asked, bemused.

"I came here to Sherwood myself to find out if the stories of a man who steals from the rich and gives to the poor are true." He looked directly at Robin. "Are they?"

Robin smiled and said, "Do you see the deer to the far side of the glen, near full hidden by the elm?" He drew his arrow.

"I barely see his antlers, in truth," the man responded. "No man alive could take down a stag at that distance."

Robin turned to his men and laughed. "Could a dead man?" And with that, the arrow flew and found its mark in the deer's breast.

"Ho!" exclaimed the man. "You *are* Robin of Locksley."

"I am, and I lead the freemen of the greenwood that you seek."

The tall man laughed out loud and took Robin's hand. "By Jove, this is a glorious day, indeed. I am John Little, and I wish to live as a freeman and not under the thumb of the Sheriff of Nottingham."

"John Little!" Will Stuteley exclaimed, suppressing a laugh. "There is nothing little about you. You should be called 'Little John' instead."

"Call me what you like," said John, "only call me 'friend.'"

"And so we shall if you love Prince Richard, the rightful heir to King Henry's throne, and desire freedom for all Englishmen," Robin said.

"I do," declared Little John.

"And so bind yourself to me and the freemen of the greenwood."

"I do."

Robin clasped him by the shoulder, and his men cheered. "Come, let us celebrate this friendship," Robin said to Little John. "Will you journey deeper into the forest with us?"

"Where you lead, I follow," Little John responded heartily.

They set off farther into the woods where a bonfire was lit and the stag was skinned and divided for cooking. Every man had a share, mugs were filled with wine, Robin played a harp he had looted from a wealthy lord, and their laughter and songs filled Sherwood Forest.

CHAPTER SIX

As the years progressed more and more men came to join Robin's merry band of outlaws. And tales of the freemen of the greenwood were told more and more often among the townsfolk in the quiet of their homes. People whispered the name Robin of Locksley with reverence. A washerwoman had found a gold piece underneath her wash pile. A farmer whose crop had been stolen by the Sheriff's men woke to find fresh deer meat at the doorstep to feed his family. And the children of the village told of a tree they were playing beneath that rained gold coins. When they looked up, they spied a man dressed all in green with a hood, laughing.

Early one evening, as Robin sat with his men in camp, one of his sentries brought what appeared to be a prisoner before him.

"I found this straggler in the woods claiming to be looking for the freemen of the greenwood. He says his name is Gilbert of Blois," said the sentry. He held out the straggler's short sword. "He came with this."

Robin looked at the sword and then at Gilbert. He was a slight youth with a large nest of thick blond hair and a vibrant glow about the cheeks. Gilbert seemed ill at ease and nervously rubbed at his chin. He kept his eyes cast downward.

"A sword, eh?" Robin said with a hint of amusement in his voice. "Archery is like breathing to me, Will Stuteley has shown me how to wrestle, and Little John has taught me to swing a cudgel. But I have not had much practice with the short sword."

Gilbert of Blois stepped forward and took back his sword. "Let us begin the lesson then," he said.

Ever ready for a challenge, Robin grasped a sword from Will Scarlett just in time to defend himself from Gilbert's first thrust. The clang of metal striking metal rang throughout the woods, and soon all of Robin's men gathered around to watch.

Although Gilbert was not nearly as large or strong as Robin, he was nimble and light-footed. As he swung his sword around again, he caught Robin off guard. Robin staggered to regain his footing while Gilbert kept him guessing as to where his next thrust would land.

Knowing that he was being bested in front of his men, Robin attempted to distract his opponent by asking, "Have we not met before, Gilbert of Blois?"

"Indeed we have," Gilbert replied with a sly smile. "And you said that we would meet again soon, yet some time has already gone by."

Robin, sensing an opening, lunged, hoping at last to have caught his opponent off guard. But Gilbert of Blois was too quick. He gracefully stepped aside and, with a flick of his wrist, nicked Robin on the back of his hand. Robin flinched. A drop of blood rose on his knuckle.

"I can see you are adept with the sword," he said. "Perhaps you will stay with us and teach me what you know."

"Aye," said Gilbert. "You have much to learn, Robin o' th' Hood."

Robin's eyes grew wide and his heart began to pound. He had been called that name only once before.

"Marian," he whispered. He saw from the smile on the youth's lips that he was right.

The men of the greenwood grew still when they saw the victor lower his sword before Robin.

"Freemen of the greenwood," Robin said to them. "Standing before me is one I have desired since first I laid eyes on her." And with that, he pushed aside Gilbert of Blois's blond wig with the tip of his sword and let it fall to the ground. Maid Marian's raven-black hair tumbled down onto her shoulders, and the men gasped.

"I still have the handkerchief you gave me on Nottingham Green," Robin said, taking the white linen cloth out from within his leather jerkin.

"It did not bring you luck today," she said with a smile, taking it from him and gently wrapping the handkerchief around his cut. "But, then again, you need more than luck to best me at the short sword."

The freemen hooted at Maid Marian's teasing. And Robin joined them.

Marian and Robin walked off into the woods where they could talk privately. Marian wasted little time in telling Robin of the danger he was in, for this was why she had come.

"Robin, the Sheriff has promised ten gold coins for the life of any one of your men, and a hundred gold coins for your head. If the people of Nottingham so much as mention the name 'Robin of Locksley,' they are thrown into jail."

"Then they will need to call me by another name," Robin smiled. He thought for a moment before exclaiming, "Robin o' th' Hood!"

"Shorter," she said. "So that the people remember. How does the name 'Robin Hood' sound to your ear?"

"Robin Hood," Robin repeated, trying it out. "Robin Hood it is. Tell anyone who wishes to join my freemen of the greenwood to ask for Robin Hood."

"I will. But I must return home now, before I am missed," said Marian, placing the blond wig back upon her head. "Be careful, Robin. For a hundred gold coins, I fear that even one of your own men could betray you," she warned before she kissed him and disappeared into the darkness of the evening.

CHAPTER SEVEN

*L*ife continued on in Sherwood Forest much the same after Marian's visit. If a rich traveler wandered through his forest, Robin and his merry band were sure to relieve him of his purse and distribute the money to the poor. Children couldn't pass a single tree without glancing up into the leaves hopefully. And the stories of the generosity of the freemen of the greenwood continued to spread throughout the countryside.

Robin told his men of the price put on his head by the Sheriff. The men were aghast, and all swore loyalty to him again. He thought little of it until one morning in early autumn, when Robin woke to find Stuteley gently shaking his arm.

"Robin," Stuteley whispered so as not to wake the other men. "Both Roger the cook and Little John are missing."

"Missing?" Robin asked, wiping the sleep from his eyes. "What do you mean?"

"Allan-a-Dale saw them stealing off, one after the other, while it was still dark. And when they were still absent when the sun rose, I thought you should know immediately."

Robin sat up at once. "Do you think they've deserted us?"

"I don't know. I more fear that they'll betray you. There's been some talk among the men after you told them about the price on your head," Stuteley said. "They'll need to be found at once."

"You're right, my friend," Robin said, springing to his feet. "I trust your thoughts as much as my own. I'll search high and low for Little John and Roger. They bound themselves to me and our cause, and I'll find out if they have truly broken their word."

"I'll come with you, Robin," Stuteley said. "For I too have a thirst for adventure, and where you go, I go too."

"Will, you're more help remaining here and leading the men in my absence. I won't return until I have news of Little John and Roger. Don't leave the forest—the Sheriff's men patrol the outside of it," Robin said, already running down the dell. "There will be time for adventure, and enough for both of us."

CHAPTER EIGHT

As Robin made his way to Nottingham he spied a large man kneeling along the river by St. Dunstan's Chapel. He ran toward him, hoping it was Little John, but as he came closer, he saw that it was a monk filling his flask. The monk was whistling.

Disappointed, Robin greeted the monk, nonetheless. "It sounds as though you are a happy priest," he said.

"I have God to go with me," replied the monk.

"I have met many men of the cloth," Robin said, pausing as the man stood. "And some had more gold than God. Perhaps you would hand over your money purse so I can check."

"Tsk! Tsk!" replied the monk. "Such is not the case with Friar Tuck."

"A churchman without a few gold coins in his own pocket from the poor box?" Robin asked skeptically. "Then perhaps you can offer me another service."

"I am at your service," Friar Tuck said, folding his hands. "Perhaps a prayer for your poor manners."

"Nay, good Tuck," replied Robin. "I wish to cross this river without wetting my feet. Would you be like St. Christopher and carry me across?"

"Of course," said Tuck. "I am a good Christian. I would ask only that you leave your knife on this side. I can throw it to you when I've returned."

Robin agreed and Friar Tuck took Robin upon his back and carried him through the stream. When Robin was set down safely on the opposite bank, Friar Tuck turned to him with a request of his own.

"Good fellow, I have carried you here. Would you grant me a favor and return me on your back? I have left my prayer book and my beads on the opposite shore." Robin could scarcely say no, for the friar was not a small man, and if it came to blows, Robin was not sure he would win.

So the friar mounted Robin's back and they returned across the river.

"Very good, Friar," said Robin. "But I am back where I began, and I still need to be across the river. And this time I think I shall bring along my knife, so that I need not return."

And as Robin bent to pick up his knife the monk charged at him and tossed him into the water. Then he leaped on top of Robin, thrashing him with his fists. "Here's what you get for trying to thieve a gentle monk!" he shouted as he hit Robin again. Then he grabbed Robin by the collar and thrust his head under the water.

After a few moments he let Robin up for a quick breath. "Who is this who would take from God's servant?" he demanded.

Robin, coughing up water, sputtered. "I am . . ." He drew a breath. "Robin . . . Hood."

"Robin Hood!" repeated the friar. He heaved the sopping Robin upon the bank and said, "I have heard of you. Tell me, good Robin, is it true that you thieve from the rich and proud and give to the lowly?"

Robin nodded, ringing the water out of his tunic.

"Well, sir," said Friar Tuck, taking off his dry cowl and placing it over Robin's shivering shoulders, "any man who looks after the poor as you do is a brother of mine. I am in your debt."

"Then I ask another favor of you," Robin said. "Loan me your cowl so that I may pass unrecognized through Nottingham."

And after the two new friends finished talking, Robin struck out on his own, dressed in the disguise of a wandering monk.

On the night that he left Sherwood Forest, Little John had awakened to see Roger slipping silently away from the camp when the others were asleep.

Little John followed Roger all the way to the front gate of Nottingham's castle. In the darkness before dawn he watched Roger approach several soldiers who were warming themselves before a fire. He could not make out what was said between the soldiers and Roger, but it was not long before they ushered Roger through the castle gate.

So he *is* going to betray Robin! Little John realized. With the front gate momentarily unattended, he slipped in unnoticed and kept to the shadows, making his way toward the Sheriff's residence.

The front door to the Sheriff's living quarters was well guarded, so Little John followed the smell of cooking potatoes around the back to the kitchen. He sneaked in and discreetly began working among the large number of cooks preparing breakfast for the castle. When no one was watching, Little John slid a large iron ladle up his sleeve. Silently he slipped into the dining hall and there found Roger waiting to speak to the Sheriff when he arrived for breakfast.

Little John attacked him savagely. "You, you, traitor!" he sputtered. "How dare you betray Robin!" he shouted, chasing Roger around the table. Pitchers and plates and serving trays clanged upon the stone floor. Little John took a swipe at Roger with the ladle and knocked him to the ground. But his yells woke the castle. Soldiers, servants, and washwomen scurried every which way, lighting torches and searching the dining hall.

But it was too late. Little John, confident that he had taught Roger a lesson, dashed out of the castle and fled from Nottingham.

The next day Lord Carfax galloped into the castle courtyard. The Sheriff was feeding his falcon, which was perched upon his gloved hand.

"King Henry is dead!" Carfax exclaimed as he dismounted his horse. "The news has just now arrived from London."

"Is he?" the Sheriff asked, pondering the implications of the royal death. He handed his falcon over to Roger, who was still nursing the bruise he had received from Little John. "Then Prince John will ride to London to take the throne."

"And the road leads right past Nottingham," Carfax added. "Wouldn't it be a befitting gift to the new king to give him the head of the outlaw, Robin of Locksley?"

The edges of the Sheriff's mouth rose in a devilish grin. "Indeed. The prince would be delighted."

"We will need bait to draw Robin of Locksley out into the open," Roger interrupted.

"Who is this?" Carfax asked curtly, glancing at the bruised man.

"This, my dear Carfax, is the man who, for one hundred gold pieces, will lead us to Robin of Locksley," the Sheriff said with satisfaction, reaching over and stroking his falcon.

"Perhaps an archery tournament next Saturday, a fair in honor of the prince, will flush this Robin out from the forest?" Carfax suggested.

"Yes," the Sheriff replied, nodding his head slowly. "But he knows there is a price on his head, so he'll be wary of showing himself."

"Allow me to make a suggestion," Roger said, leaning toward the two men. "He loves the one called Marian Fitzwalter."

"Does he?" The Sheriff looked gleeful. "Arrest her and bring her to me!"

"How dare you betray Robin!" he shouted, chasing Roger around the table.

CHAPTER NINE

*D*ays went by and still Robin could find neither Little John nor Roger, though he had walked the southernmost reaches of Sherwood. Shortly before noon on a cold October day, he came upon a group of knights traveling through Sherwood toward Nottingham. Leading them was a tall knight in the strangest armor Robin had ever seen. It was coal black with gold inscriptions, silver chain mail, and palm leaf etchings covering its surface. Robin slipped the cowl he was wearing over his head, drew his bow, and stepped before the men. The element of surprise was his, and before any of them could unsheathe a sword or string a bow, Robin was upon them.

"Ho, there, Black Knight," Robin began. "I see you are heading toward Nottingham."

"Do you always draw your arrow on simple travelers journeying through these parts?" the Black Knight asked, pulling up on his horse's reins.

"A 'simple traveler' does not dress in such finery," Robin countered, eyeing the bulging money purse that hung from the knight's belt. "If I had to guess, I would venture that the money you carry is for the Sheriff of Nottingham."

"If you tell me your name, highwayman," said the knight calmly, "I will tell you why I journey to Nottingham."

"I am afraid my name has become a dangerous one," Robin replied. "And the information will cost you what is in your purse."

The Black Knight untied his purse and tossed it to Robin. Robin opened the bag: There was more gold there than he had seen in an entire year. He immediately suspected a trap and scanned the forest for soldiers. But the woods were still. Assured that none of the Sheriff's men lurked behind the hedgerows waiting to pounce, he pushed back his cowl and answered the knight's question.

"I am a friend to the rightful heir to the English throne," Robin said proudly. "And this money could feed a good many of his subjects."

"Has news of the throne not reached you here in the forest?" the Black Knight asked. "King Henry has died this very week."

"Oh no! Then Prince John . . ."

"May take the throne within a fortnight," the dark knight interjected. "He is traveling to Nottingham today on his way to London."

"Are you going there to join him or stop him?" Robin asked.

"I am here to seek someone who is said to steal from the rich and give to the poor."

One of the knights made a motion to remove his sword from its scabbard, but Robin quickly dropped the money purse and leveled his drawn arrow at him. The soldier took his hand from the sword's handle.

"He is also reported to be the greatest archer in all of England," the dark knight continued. "Perhaps I will see his skill at the archery tournament being held tomorrow at the Nottingham Fair."

"Nay, good knight, he would be a fool to travel to that place. No doubt the town is full of Prince John's soldiers."

"They say," the knight added, "that the hand of a fair maid is being offered to the best archer."

"A maiden? What is her name?"

"Marian Fitzwalter, the daughter of an old friend of mine. Do you know of her?"

"My beloved!" Robin gasped. And before the knight had a chance to question him further, Robin raced into the woods.

CHAPTER TEN

*T*he morning of the fair broke cold and windy. The Sheriff of Nottingham's pennants, covered with the emblem of a falcon and dagger, snapped in the wind high above the city green. The villagers congregated upon the green to witness the tournament, and to see Prince John, the man who would be king.

But the fair didn't draw only villagers. Robin, with his friar's cowl pulled over his head, was among them. He walked on the fringes of the crowd, carefully watching as the Sheriff's men set up the archery field. Nearly a hundred soldiers were scattered about the area, by Robin's count. And not all of them were the Sheriff's. Robin thought it peculiar that there were so many soldiers for a simple tournament. Then he realized they must be there to ensnare him.

A quarterstaff match was being fought at the edge of the green, and Robin wove through the crowd cheering the match. While the wealthy lords and ladies watched, engrossed in the competition, he cut their purse strings with his knife. He removed the money and, backing away from the match, doled it out without fanfare to the children who were chasing each other through the crowd.

When he handed a gold coin to a boy in a threadbare cloak, the boy looked at it, then asked happily, "Who do I have to thank for this?"

"Robin Hood," Robin replied softly.

"The outlaw?" the boy asked eagerly.

Robin held a finger to his lips, said "Shhhh!" and moved on.

At last the archery field was ready. Trumpets blared and the drawbridge to Nottingham Castle was lowered. The Sheriff rode out first on his black steed, his falcon perched menacingly upon his left hand. Behind him was Lord Carfax,

A quarterstaff match was being fought at the edge of the green . . .

whose longbow was slung across his chest. Trailing them was Maid Marian riding an old spotted mare. On either side of her walked an armed escort. Behind her rode Roger the turncoat.

The trumpets sounded again, and a gilded gold carriage rolled across the drawbridge. In it was Prince John, and when the people saw him for the first time, they laughed aloud at his fussy bright-red velvet cape and feminine white gloves.

"Peasants!" he sneered dismissively, drawing the French lace across the coach's windows.

When the prince's carriage reached the viewing stand, the soldiers who followed him fanned out around the archery field. Prince John mounted the stand and joined the Sheriff.

"We are pleased that you are able to join us today for what will surely be a grand exhibition of the county's finest marksmen," the Sheriff said to the prince, bowing grandly.

"I came," Prince John said haughtily, "to see you capture the outlaw who lives in Sherwood. I will be crowned king early next week and will not allow my kingdom to be threatened by him and his band of thieves."

"I assure you, he will be here," the Sheriff said placatingly. "A robin will always return to its nest if its mate is there." He glanced at Marian, who sat pale and silent in her seat.

Then the Sheriff stood. "The prize, today," he announced to the several dozen contestants who had gathered on the field, bows in hand, "is the hand of Maid Marian Fitzwalter." He held up her ring, and the archers smiled. Marian was without doubt the prettiest woman in the land.

The Sheriff then turned to the prince. "Each archer will be allowed three shots to determine if they will proceed to the next round," the Sheriff said, explaining the rules of the tournament to him. "And before this day is out, we shall capture

Robin of Locksley. He will no doubt be one of the men competing for this ring, if he is as good an archer as the people say he is."

Prince John scowled and moved about uncomfortably in his seat. "It is cold and windy, and I do not wish to be here all day," the prince told the Sheriff impatiently. He reached over and snatched Marian's ring from the Sheriff's hand. "Take this ring," he instructed the guard closest to him, "tie it to a ribbon, and hang it from the limb of that elm at the far side of the green. The man who fires an arrow through it will be your Robin of Locksley."

"That is an impossible shot," the Sheriff protested.

"And I am an uncomfortable man," snapped Prince John. The guard began to trot toward the tree when a gust of wind shook the tent surrounding the viewing stand. The prince shivered, then called the guard back. He grabbed the ribbon from his hand, and in a booming voice declared, "Thread this maid's ring with your arrow, and you shall receive her." He took off his own golden ring, heated a measure of sealing wax over a nearby warming fire, and poured it on the ribbon. He then pressed the top of his ring into the wax, leaving an impression of the royal seal on it. He held it out for the competitors to see, and announced with a flourish, "Any man who breaks my seal with a stray arrow will receive death."

Prince John handed the ribbon and ring to his guard, who marched it across the field. He turned to the Sheriff and added, "This should narrow the field."

The archers took one look at the new target and decided that their lives were worth more to them than Marian's hand. All but two backed away from the village green and the archery competition.

"Where are your suitors now?" the Sheriff said to Marian. "It seems that you are not as desirable as you once appeared. Only two men remain. One is Lord Carfax, and I suspect that the one in the hooded cape is your Robin."

The Sheriff smiled as he watched Marian grow even paler, for he knew the cause: Robin had returned and risked certain capture and death for her.

CHAPTER ELEVEN

*T*he Sheriff of Nottingham rested his cawing falcon upon a wooden perch and walked out upon the archery field, drawing his cape tightly around him. When he reached Carfax and the hooded archer, he said, "The target has been set. See the ring on yonder tree? If your arrow strays and hits the prince's royal seal, you shall receive death. Are the rules understood?"

"Yes," Carfax answered.

The Sheriff waited for a reply from the other archer, but when he received only a nod of the head, he said bitterly, "As you will, say nothing. Lord Carfax will shoot first." He left the field and returned to the viewing stand, taking his seat between Prince John and Maid Marian.

"I can easily outshoot a common thief," Carfax said to his hooded competitor. "This will be as easy as burning down Locksley Manor." He peered at his rival but received no reaction to his prodding. With deliberate slowness he drew an arrow from his quiver and smoothed its feathers.

"When I pierce the ring with this arrow, I will have taken from you everything you have always desired," Carfax said, his tone venomous. "First your house, your lands, your whole inheritance, then your mother, and . . ."—here he drew back the arrow and aimed—"now the title of the greatest archer in England and the hand of your beloved, Marian."

He released the ashen wand and it sailed true, straight toward Marian's ring. But the wind shifted its course at the last moment, and the arrow swayed, merely nicking the ring as it buried itself in the tree's trunk. The ring swung out widely as it was struck, then gently rebounded against the side of Carfax's arrow.

Marian sighed with relief as Carfax cursed, "There is too much wind!"

The hooded archer looked from the tree trunk to Carfax to the trunk again. Then he lifted his bow and picked an arrow from the quiver on his back.

"You will not hit that target," Carfax hissed. "But if you do, you will reveal yourself."

The archer waited a moment, glanced at the briskly flapping pennants, and in the instant it took for the wind to change direction by a degree, he released the arrow. The magnificent twang of the bowstring could be heard over the entire field.

The instant the dart was released, he plucked another from his quiver and sent it flying in the same direction.

Both the Sheriff and Maid Marian leaned forward in their seats.

Thwack! The first arrow pierced Prince John's royal seal and cut through the ribbon. The ring fell.

Thwack! The second arrow struck the tree, driving precisely through the gold ring as it dropped. The ring spun around the arrow.

A great cry went up among the crowd. It was the finest shot anyone had ever seen. Marian leaped to her feet. Carfax threw his own bow to the ground in fury.

The Sheriff of Nottingham, enraged, yelled, "Arrest that man! He has broken the royal crest!"

But the hooded archer did not run. Instead he stood erect and waited for the soldiers to surround him. By the point of a sword, he was led before the Sheriff's viewing stand.

"Because you have cut my royal seal," Prince John announced before the Sheriff could say anything, "you have lost the tournament. I award Marian Fitzwalter to Lord Carfax."

The archer remained impassive, but Carfax smiled broadly. "Bring her to me, Roger. We will ride to St. Dunstan's Chapel and be married before the hour is out." Roger led Marian off the viewing stand and placed her on Lord Carfax's horse.

The Sheriff now addressed the hooded archer. "What is your name, so that we may carve it on your headstone?"

The archer did not answer. Instead he seemed to be scanning the faces in the crowd.

"Do you search for your outlaw friends?" the Sheriff asked. "They won't be here. I have two dozen of my best horsemen guarding the forest. Any man who so much as sticks his head out from behind a branch will be shot."

Prince John grew impatient. "Is this Locksley?" he demanded. "Is this the leader of their troop?"

"What is your name?" the Sheriff repeated. "Is it Robin Fitzooth of Locksley Manor?"

"No longer," Robin said, casting off his cowl. "I am Robin Hood of Sherwood Forest." A hush came over the crowd. Here was the man who had helped them for so long, and here he stood in front of both the Sheriff and the prince, neither bowing nor groveling. He stood as a free man. The crowd seemed to hold a collective breath of anticipation.

"It doesn't matter what you call yourself," the Sheriff sneered. "Guards, seize him!"

But the soldiers could not take him. As if breaking from a trance, the crowd swarmed the field and surrounded the soldiers. It was as though every man, woman, and child there released all of the hatred they had felt against the Sheriff lo these many years that they lived under his oppressive rule. They tore down banners and knocked swords from soldiers' hands. In the melee, the Sheriff's falcon sprung from its perch and took flight.

"Run, Robin!" the villagers shouted. "Save yourself!"

Amidst the turmoil Robin dashed to the tree where Marian's ring still hung. He pulled his two arrows out, sheathed them in his quiver, and put the ring in his pocket. Spying another company of soldiers springing out from Nottingham Castle, Robin darted from the green.

CHAPTER TWELVE

Once again Robin found himself racing through the north gate and sprinting away from Nottingham so fast his chest ached. He was charging toward Sherwood Forest when he saw them—soldiers on horseback, with swords drawn, waiting before him, blocking his entrance to the woods.

He slowed his pace and reached for an arrow, but he knew he didn't have enough darts in his quiver to fell all the soldiers before him. He glanced back to see more men moving quickly to his left and right, blocking any escape.

It was at that moment that Robin heard the snap of a bowstring. He tensed, waiting to be struck, but instead one of the Sheriff's men fell to the ground, an arrow in his back.

And then arrow upon arrow rained down from Sherwood Forest upon the soldiers. It was the freemen of the greenwood! The horsemen began to turn around to protect themselves, but could not see where the arrows were coming from. As arrow after arrow fell, Robin dashed through the soldiers' diminishing ranks into the cover of the woods. Bounding through the trees, he was suddenly grabbed by the arm and swung around.

"What took you so long?" Stuteley said to his friend joyfully. "We were beginning to think you lost the tournament!"

Robin laughed, but then quickly looked around. Allan-a-Dale, Warrenton, Will Scarlett, Arthur-à-Bland, and the rest of the men who had sworn allegiance to his cause of freedom kept up the furious barrage of arrows against the soldiers. And among his men was Little John.

"Robin," he called out, "Roger the Cook has betrayed you!"

"So I discovered," Robin replied, slinging an arrow across his bow. "I saw him help Carfax steal away with Marian. We must make for St. Dunstan's Chapel and save Marian! Are you with me?"

"Where you lead, I follow," Little John responded heartily.

Robin shot at a soldier, then cried out to his men, "Through the dell!"

And so Robin was again leading his men through Sherwood Forest, but it was as never before. For soon the Sheriff's soldiers were upon them and with a number Robin didn't think possible. This time the arrows were flying *toward* Robin and his men.

"You go ahead," Stuteley told Robin. "We'll slow them down."

"God be with you," was all Robin said before he pushed deeper into the woods.

Though he knew the easiest and quickest paths to the chapel, the forest seemed alive with soldiers. He passed through the dell, but as he ascended the hill that led him to St. Dunstan's, he felt a sharp pang in his shoulder. He'd been struck! The arrow sliced the leather strap that held his quiver. Arrows scattered about the forest floor as Robin fell to the ground.

Wincing in pain, Robin reached around and plucked the arrow from his back. Another arrow whistled past his head. He picked up one of his arrows from the forest floor, and shot. The Sheriff's archer fell, clutching at his chest. Robin snatched up his peacock arrow in time to see the Sheriff charging at him, riding high in the saddle with his falcon flying overhead.

Robin slung the peacock arrow across his bow, and whispered, "As you once flew at Prince Richard's heart, now find the heart of the Sheriff of Nottingham." He slowly took aim, following the figure of the Sheriff as he rode.

The destination of the arrow was certain; never had Robin had such a clear shot. But just as he was about to let the arrow fly, the Sheriff's falcon swooped from above, knocking Robin off balance, burying its talons into his wounded shoulder, and shaking his aim. The arrow fired low and hit the Sheriff's horse.

The horse whinnied and fell, throwing the Sheriff from the saddle. The Sheriff scrambled to his feet and scurried back to his horse, only to find that it was dead. Then he saw it—the famed arrow of Richard the Lionheart. It was half buried in the horse's chest. With a violent yank he pulled it out and headed up the hill.

Robin shook himself free of the falcon and continued running toward the chapel. As he was about to crest the hill, he heard the twang of a bowstring. A searing pain ran from his arm, up his shoulder, and through his entire body as an arrow pierced his forearm and imbedded itself into the tree beside him. Frantically, he tried to remove it from the tree and free his arm, when he caught sight of the Sheriff coming up behind him, stringing another arrow across his bow.

Desperate, Robin snapped the arrow, releasing his arm. But when he looked at the arrow, he saw that it was tipped with peacock feathers. Prince Richard's arrow! Robin stared at it in horror. Could it be that he truly had lost everything: his house and lands, his mother, Marian, and now the arrow Richard had entrusted to his father and that his father had entrusted to him?

Robin looked at the Sheriff in such bewilderment that the Sheriff paused for a moment. Then the Sheriff grinned demonically. He drew back his arrow slowly, savoring his victory over Robin, until the bow could stand no more tension.

Then he released the bowstring.

CHAPTER THIRTEEN

*R*obin closed his eyes, but the Sheriff's arrow, shot not twenty feet from where Robin stood, never hit him. Instead, he heard it cut into the earth an inch from his leg.

Robin looked up, only to see the Sheriff of Nottingham fall. In his back was a still-quivering arrow. It was a peacock arrow! Robin blinked. What did this mean? In his hand he held the broken peacock arrow. Where could this second one have come from?

Robin staggered to his feet, clutching his bleeding hand. Just then the knight in coal black armor whom he had met upon the road the day before galloped up the hill with his men behind him. And suddenly Robin knew where the second peacock arrow had come from.

"Good knight," Robin said as the Black Knight drew near, "you have a peacock arrow!"

"And you have a wedding to attend," replied the Black Knight, smiling mysteriously. "Now, take my hand and you shall ride with me."

Robin burst through the door at St. Dunstan's Chapel. Carfax, about to finish the vows that would wed him to Marian, picked up his bow, but before he had time to reach his quiver, Robin sent an arrow through his throat. The soldiers who held Robin's beloved shrank back. Marian gasped.

"You have desecrated my church," the Bishop of Hereford cried out, dropping his Bible.

"Quiet, scoundrel, or you'll be next!" the Black Knight roared. "You no longer have the Sheriff to protect you."

"Marian," Robin exclaimed, running to her.

"Robin," Marian cried. "A moment longer and I would have been lost to you forever." She gently reached for his arm to inspect his injury. He had wrapped the linen handkerchief she had given him years ago around the wound, but still it bled. "I haven't another linen scarf to bind this with," she said.

"Take mine," the Black Knight spoke up, handing her his kerchief. Then he addressed Robin. "I am impressed, forester. I watched you in secret upon the green, and then in the forest where you chose to fight instead of surrender. I did not know such men still existed in England. For you see, I have been out of the country for a spell."

"Good knight," Marian interrupted. "I do not wish to appear rude, but Robin's wounds need to be bound."

"I agree. This brave man needs to be bound . . . bound in matrimony!" The Black Knight laughed. "Here is your beloved, here about us is a chapel. All we need is a priest."

The Bishop of Hereford shied away. "I would not perform this ceremony for the outlaw if my very soul depended upon it."

"I'll gladly do it," came a voice from the back of the chapel.

"Friar Tuck," Robin called happily.

"I heard the screech of a falcon from my abbey cell not a quarter mile from here," the friar said cheerily. "I thought it worthwhile to investigate."

Robin smiled at the kindly friar but said, "Long ago I bound myself to Prince Richard, the rightful heir to the crown, and the cause of freedom. And I can not break that sacred pledge and bind myself to a wife until he returns from the Holy Land to release me from it."

"Then consider yourself unbound," said the Black Knight.

Robin looked puzzled. "What do you mean?"

"The kerchief," the Black Knight said. "Look at the kerchief."

Marian unwound it carefully and gasped. Upon the linen cloth were the images of three lions on a scarlet field—Richard the Lionheart's emblem.

Robin looked up at the knight in disbelief. "Prince Richard?" he asked.

"I am," was the reply.

"Sire, long have I fought in your service," Robin said. "But I have broken the arrow you entrusted to my father."

"Your father was a great soldier and a good friend," the prince said. "When I heard he had died, it grieved my heart greatly. But then I began to hear rumors of a lover of freedom even greater than my old friend William Fitzooth, named Robin Hood. A man who stole from the rich and proud and gave to the poor and lowly."

"Your faithful servant, Your Highness," Robin replied, bowing deeply.

"You shall have your peacock arrow back, Robin of Locksley and Sherwood Forest. Before I left the Holy Land, I had another made, because the first brought me such good fortune. You have served me well, and I now unbind you from your pledge. You are a free man, and free to marry this charming maid."

Soon all of Robin's men gathered at the chapel. Friar Tuck performed the wedding ceremony, Prince Richard the Lionheart served as Robin's best man, and Stuteley climbed the small tower of the chapel to ring the bells. The greenwood rang with their sound.

The wedding party returned to Nottingham Castle behind Prince Richard. Roger, the traitor, had hidden in the castle's kitchen when the villagers rebelled. He was found and tossed into the dungeon as were numerous other lords who had been loyal to Prince John.

The banquet hall was thrown open, and a great feast was held in honor of the newlyweds. Robin played the harp for his new wife as Little John sang with a voice that filled the hall. And there was laughter and ale and songs long into the morning.

Robin played the harp for his new wife as Little John sang with a voice that filled the hall.

The news of Richard's return to England spread over the countryside like wildflowers in spring. The freedom that had been denied to Englishmen returned when Richard took the throne. The villagers were repaid what had been stolen from them, and land taken by the Sheriff and Prince John was returned to its rightful owners. To prove his magnanimity in his triumph, King Richard called Prince John before him, and in an act of brotherly affection, pardoned him for the crime of trying to usurp the throne.

Friar Tuck was offered the position of Bishop of Hereford to replace the previous bishop. But he did not accept. He preferred the open road, a simple chapel, and life in the wild among the animals.

Little John found work in the kitchen at nearby Tickhill Castle. He was frequently called from the kettle and the fire to entertain the lords and ladies of the castle with songs of his days with the famous Robin Hood.

Stuteley, an orphan from an early age, had nowhere to go when the merry band of Sherwood Forest went their separate ways. Robin, in affection for his trusted friend, gave to him the lands of Locksley. Warrenton, who had fought beside Robin these many years, returned with Stuteley as chief forester of the property.

Robin stayed in Nottingham, where King Richard bequeathed upon him the position of Sheriff. He and Marian lived a life of simplicity, seeking justice for all in the county. They were happy, and the people were happy to have the brave Robin Hood as their Sheriff.

At the end of a long life Marian kissed her husband good night then died quietly in her sleep. Robin found little to live for once his beloved had passed from the earth. For the last time he gathered his men to him at the castle in

He drew forth his cherished peacock arrow. . . .

Nottingham. When they came to his chamber, he drew forth his cherished peacock arrow, whose bright colors had faded with time, and slung it across his bow. The twang of the string struck a pain in the hearts of the freemen of the greenwood as they saw Robin fall amongst his pillows.

"Bury my body and Marian's where that arrow lands, my friends. My soul is now free." With those words, he breathed his last.

The arrow flew from the castle window and arched upward into the blue English sky, where it was caught by the wind. The breeze lifted it higher, as though taking it into its hand and leading it deeper into the forest.

As the peacock arrow began its descent and returned to earth, all of Sherwood lay before it, green and alive and free.